...fferent way and at his or her own ...between reading levels and read favorite books again and again. Others read through each level in order. You can help your young reader improve and become more confident by encouraging his or her own interests and abilities. From books your child reads with you to the first books he or she reads alone, there are I Can Read Books for every stage of reading:

**SHARED READING**
Basic language, word repetition, and whimsical illustrations, ideal for sharing with your emergent reader

**BEGINNING READING**
Short sentences, familiar words, and simple concepts for children eager to read on their own

**READING WITH HELP**
Engaging stories, longer sentences, and language play for developing readers

**READING ALONE**
Complex plots, challenging vocabulary, and high-interest topics for the independent reader

**ADVANCED READING**
Short paragraphs, chapters, and exciting themes for the perfect bridge to chapter books

**I Can Read Books** have introduced children to the joy of reading since 1957. Featuring award-winning authors and illustrators and a fabulous cast of beloved characters, I Can Read Books set the standard for beginning readers.

A lifetime of discovery begins with the magical words **"I Can Read!"**

*Visit www.icanread.com for information on enriching your child's reading experience.*

HARP38963
 For information address HarperCollins Children's Books, a division of HarperCollins Publishers, 195 Broadway, New York, NY 10007.
www.icanread.com
ISBN 978-0-06-236095-3
Book design by Erica De Chavez

17 18 19 20 21 LSCC 10 9 8 7 6 5 4 3 2

❖

First Edition

# BATGIRL™

by Liz Marsham
pictures by Lee Ferguson

HARPER
*An Imprint of* HarperCollins*Publishers*

Barbara Gordon climbs through
her bedroom window.
She's been out fighting crime
in Gotham City.
She is secretly Batgirl.

Barbara checks her Utility Belt.

She has all of her tools.

But something is missing.

A bag hangs open and empty.

The present she got

for her father is gone!

Barbara's father is Gotham City Police Commissioner James Gordon. They're meeting for breakfast in a few hours.

She has to find the present
before then.
Barbara heads back out
into the night to retrace her steps.

Batgirl swings down into an alley.
She stopped a robbery there
earlier that night.
She looks around the alley
and into the shadows,
but everything is quiet now.

It wasn't so quiet before!
Two robbers were trying
to take money from a family.
Batgirl threw a smoke bomb.
The cloud covered the alley
and distracted the robbers.

Batgirl swung down on her Batrope
and knocked the robbers
into a Dumpster.

She wonders if the missing
present fell in the Dumpster.
Batgirl peeks inside.
All she sees is trash.

Batgirl thinks about
where she went next.
She remembers talking to a fan
as they stood on a street corner.

The fan wanted to have her picture taken with Batgirl.
She wonders if the present fell out of her bag while she posed.

Batgirl searches
the street corner.
She doesn't see
the present anywhere.

But she does meet some new fans!

Batgirl poses for a photo with them.

Suddenly, Batgirl remembers
what happened next.
A large truck was
speeding down the street.

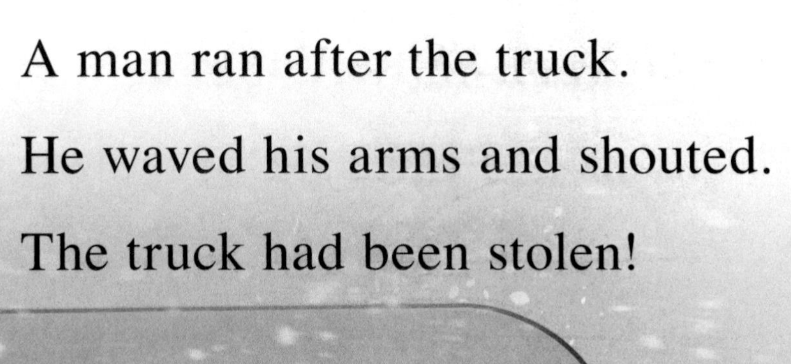

A man ran after the truck.

He waved his arms and shouted.

The truck had been stolen!

Batgirl revved her Batcycle.

She raced after the stolen truck.

She wonders if the present
was left behind
when she rode off on her Batcycle.

Batgirl searches the street
where she chased the truck.
The present isn't there.

The owner of the truck
waves to Batgirl.
She asks him
if he saw the present.
He hasn't, but he gives her
a free hot chocolate.

Batgirl remembers following
the robbers to the park
after they left the truck.
She wonders if the present
is somewhere in the park.

She spied on the gang.
When they saw her,
they ran away.

The gang ran past a fountain.
Batgirl caught up to them quickly.
The gang didn't want to be caught.
They stopped running
and turned to face the hero.
They were going to fight Batgirl.

Batgirl is an expert
at martial arts.
Each of the gang members
gave their best effort.

The last gang member
was the best fighter.
But Batgirl bounced off a tree
to avoid his attack.
She won the fight easily
and tied up the gang.

Now Batgirl looks around the park.

She heads for the tree.

The present is in the tree!
Batgirl is glad she found it.
She races home
to surprise her dad
with his birthday present!

Barbara is very tired.
But her dad's birthday
is a success.
When Batgirl is on the case,
everybody wins!